ANOTHER CUB SCOUT BOOK BY

Henry Gregor Felsen

CUB SCOUT AT LAST!

ILLUSTRATED
BY Paul Galdone

# Anyone

# for

# CUB

# SCOUTS?

by
Henry Gregor Felsen

Charles Scribner's Sons    New York

LIBRARY OF CONGRESS CATALOG CARD NO. 54-5923

# Contents

# Contents

Anyone for CUB SCOUTS?

# Chapter 1

## A NEW
## PLACE TO LIVE

When Scotty woke up he knew he was in his own house, in his own room, and in his own bed. Yet the moment he opened his eyes he was so homesick he groaned aloud.

It was Scotty's first morning in the new house, and if you have ever moved to a new neighborhood or a different town, you know just how he felt.

Everything was wrong. The ceiling was the wrong shape, the window overlooked the wrong view, the closet was in the wrong place.

Even familiar things were wrong. His bed was against the wrong wall, his dresser faced the wrong way, and his toys and tools were in the wrong corner, seeming to be as lost in this strange house as Scotty himself.

Scotty heard footsteps coming toward his room. They sounded the same as on other mornings, but there was something different about them. They came from the wrong direction.

When the footsteps reached his door, Scotty looked up guardedly. He was almost surprised to find that his mother still looked the same.

"Breakfast in ten minutes, Scotty," his mother said.

Scotty sighed loudly. "I'll be ready, Mom." He tried to sound cheerful, but somehow the words came out in a slow, mournful parade.

When he had washed and dressed, Scotty went into the new kitchen. There was a little breakfast nook with built-in benches and a table with a bright red top.

"Isn't this a pleasant place to eat?" Scotty's mother said. "We didn't have a nice place like this in our old kitchen. You'll like it."

Scotty slid under the table and perched on the smooth leather-like covering on the bench. He missed his old chair that he could move just where he wanted it. The bench was the wrong distance from the table, and that made breakfast all wrong.

"Don't you think this is a lovely house?" Scotty's mother asked as she put a glass of orange juice before him.

"I guess so," Scotty said. But he was thinking that it was a strange house, and he felt like a visitor in it.

"This is a very nice town," Scotty's mother said. "I know you'll like it better than the place we used to live."

Scotty choked on his orange juice. *No* place could be nicer than the town they had moved from. It was disloyal of his mother to say the new town was better. He could prove she was wrong.

Scotty sipped his orange juice and made a horrible face. It didn't taste like orange juice at all. It tasted like gasoline or something. Some town they had moved to! Didn't even have good orange juice!

Scotty's mother brought his usual toast and eggs. Scotty eyed the food disdainfully. The bread they sold in this new town didn't make good toast at all. And the eggs didn't look nearly as good as the eggs he used to eat. A *fine* town they had moved to.

"Have you looked at our nice yard?" Scotty's mother asked, sitting opposite him. "It has a wonderful tree to climb. Dad might help you build a tree house in it. You've always wanted a tree house."

Scotty looked out of the window at the tree and yard. It was a dumb tree. It didn't have sense enough to have the right kind of branches for climbing or building a tree house. It wasn't half as good as the tree they'd left behind. Not *half* as half as good.

"You're not eating." Scotty's mother said.

Scotty sighed again. "I guess I'm not very hungry this morning."

"That's because you still feel strange here," Scotty's mother said cheerfully. "But you'll feel at home in a few days, and you'll be your old self again. Once you get used to the house, and meet new friends, you'll never want to leave this place."

His mother talked on about how nice their new home would be, but Scotty hardly heard what she was saying. He was thinking, and dreaming.

If he were still in his old home he'd be hearing some familiar voices at the back door by now. Fred and Gary would be there on their bikes, and he'd be dashing out to join them. They'd be off for a ride to the creek to hunt for minnows, or going over to the park to play ball, or working on that racing car they had started to build.

If it was a Tuesday Fred and Gary might already be wearing their Cub Scout shirts and neckerchiefs, and he would be wearing his, because their Den met in the summer too. That meant a Den meeting later

with all the other kids, and the Den projects, and songs, and the fun of working
side by side with friends he'd known all
his life.

Tuesday . . . It *was* Tuesday. Today all
his friends would be at the meeting, but
he would be missing. They would be singing and playing games and working together and talking and having fun. Without him.

A wild thought flashed into Scotty's
mind. He would run away. He would make
his way back to their old home. When his
parents found out where he was, they
would give up this new house and move
back. Then everything would be right
again.

Scotty looked at his mother. The way
she was staring at him, he was sure she

could read his thoughts. And when she spoke, he was positive.

"I know you feel strange and lost, Scotty," his mother said. "But it won't take you long to make new friends. In fact, I'll tell you what I plan to do. While you are out playing this morning, I'm going to find out where the neighborhod Cub Den meets. And once you're in a Den, you'll feel at home again."

Scotty looked thoughtful, and then he smiled. "I guess you're right, Mom," he said. "I'll never find another Den as good as the old one, but it will be a Den."

"You take your bike and look around the neighborhood," Scotty's mother said. "By the time you get back I'll be able to tell you about the Den—unless you find out first, of course."

"Okay." Scotty felt more cheerful as he left the kitchen and went to get his bike. He wheeled it around to the front of the house, and paused to consider where he should ride.

Suddenly he was aware of something. Or, actually, the lack of something.

He could see up and down his street, and along the cross street. And for as far as he could see, the streets were empty.

There were some little tiny kids, and some grown-ups, but they didn't count. There wasn't a sight or a sound of anybody around his age.

Scotty's mouth opened in a silent movement of despair. If there were any kids his age, they'd certainly be outside. It looked as though they had moved to a place where he was the only boy in the neighborhod.

## Chapter 2

## A SEARCH FOR FRIENDS

Scotty waited. He looked up the street, down the street, and across the street. If there *were* any boys of his age in the neighborhood, he'd be bound to hear or see them.

He looked, and he listened, but all he heard was the sound of a saw, and all he could see was an old man sawing at the limb of a fallen tree.

Scotty shrugged. If there weren't any boys in the neighborhood, there *was* an old man sawing a tree, and that was better

than nothing. Old men were a pretty friendly lot, and maybe this one would give him a turn with the saw.

Scotty gave his bike a push, swung into the saddle, and coasted down the street toward the old man. He braked to a stop a few feet away from the sawing place, swung off the bike, and leaned across the seat to watch.

The old man who guided the saw was lean and craggy, with high cheekbones, sharp black eyes, and a drooping moustache. He sawed with a slow, even stroke, and while he was busy, took no notice of his young visitor.

But after a few minutes the old man took his hand from the saw, straightening up, and turned slowly toward Scotty. Scotty's head lifted, and he smiled.

The old man raised his hand and pointed up the street. He said one word.

"Git."

Scotty stared. He couldn't believe his ears.

The old man gestured with his hand. "I said git."

Scotty remained speechless. He was too shocked to move.

"Boy," the old man said, "do you speak English?"

Scotty nodded.

"Do you understand it when you hear it spoken?"

Again Scotty nodded.

"Then," said the old man, "git goin'."

Scotty looked at the old man with a puzzled expression. "Why do you want to chase me away?" he asked. "I won't get in your way. I just would like to watch you."

"And about that broken window of mine?" the old man said. "What about that?"

"I don't know anything about any windows," Scotty said. "I'm new in the neighborhood."

The old man snorted. "That's what they all say. But the window didn't break itself. No sir! So I'm telling you, boy. Climb on that bicycle and git. I don't want you around."

"Honest," Scotty said. "I just moved here."

"Move, again, boy," the old man said. "And move fast. Git."

Scotty got on his bike and rode away. He couldn't understand what had happened. Somebody had broken the old man's window, but why blame it on him? And where were the other boys the old man had talked about. Who were they?

Scotty rode along slowly on his bike, hoping to see some sign of other boys, but he saw none. He was becoming more and more convinced that he was the only boy in the whole neighborhood.

The second time around the block Scotty saw a small dog playing in its yard. It was a playful pup, and the sight of it gladdened Scotty's heart. The dog ran toward the street and barked at him in a high, babyish voice.

Scotty braked his bike, leaned it on the kick stand, and walked to the dog. When he reached it, he got down on his knees and held out his hands to the small black-and-white pup.

"Here, boy," Scotty said in a friendly tone. "Come here, boy. Let's be friends."

The dog advanced toward Scotty, his tail wagging, his round eyes bright.

"Nice little dog," Scotty said, reaching out to pet the puppy. "Nice little dog."

The dog licked Scotty's hand, and Scotty picked it up in his arms, and held it to him while it tried to lick his face. For the moment Scotty forgot he was in a strange town, and without friends. He had found a little dog, and it would be his friend.

Scotty was tickling the dog behind the ears when a harsh voice broke into the pleasant play.

Scotty looked up to see a woman standing on the front porch of the house, her face red and angry.

"Put that dog down," the woman commanded. "Take your hands off him this minute."

Scotty let the puppy drop. "I only wanted to play with him a little bit," Scotty said.

"I know how you boys play!" the woman stormed. "If I could get my hands on the boy who tied that can to my dog's tail, I'd have that boy arrested!"

"I wouldn't be mean to your dog," Scotty said. "I'm new here. We just moved to this neighborhood. I . . ."

"That's what they all say," the woman scolded. "They all blame someone else. But I won't have my dog teased. If I catch you near my dog again, I'll call the police! They'll teach you boys some manners! Come here, Towser. Come away from the bad boy."

Scotty turned sadly and mounted his bike again. He hadn't seen any boys, but this was the second time he had been chased because of something that some other, invisible boys had done. It seemed that he lived in the middle of the most awful, unfriendly neighborhood in the whole wide world.

Abandoning the street, Scotty cut through several back alleys, hoping he might find some boys at play in their back yards. But again he found no sign of any boys his age.

He stopped to watch a man wash his car and was chased away.

He stopped to watch some little children playing on swings and slides and was chased by a woman who accused him of being the boy who had teased the little ones a week past.

At the end of two hours Scotty was in despair. He had been chased from a dozen places, and accused of a dozen bad things. The people acted as though they were fighting off an invasion of bad boys, yet Scotty hadn't seen a single boy.

He had been accused of all their crimes, however.

It was with a heavy heart that Scotty finally turned toward home. The house that his parents called home. And it was then that the first cheering thought of the day came into his mind.

His mother was finding out about the Cub Scouts, and as soon as she did, he would join the Den and meet the other Cubs. When that happened, his troubles would be over. He would have friends, and there would be a lot of interesting things to do.

Scotty rode home as fast as he could, eager to find out where the Den met, and when the next meeting would be. He wouldn't even have to wait for a meeting to get acquainted with the boys. Once he knew where they lived, he could visit them.

He needed friends, and he needed them right away. He was still feeling pretty bad because of the way he had been treated by the neighbors, and he was hungry for the sight of a friendly Cub face.

Scotty wheeled into his yard, put his bike into the garage, and ran into the house. "Well, Mom?" he burst out. "Where are the Cubs?"

"Did you have a nice time this morning?" his mother asked.

"Terrible," Scotty said lightly. "I didn't

see any boys, but from the way the people act around here, the place is full of boys who break windows, and tease animals and little kids. *Everybody* chased me."

"Oh?" Scotty's mother looked distressed.

"Don't worry, Mom," Scotty said. "I won't play with kids like that. I'll stick to the Cub friends I'll have. Where's the Den and when does it meet?"

Scotty's mother shook her head slowly. "I'm sorry, Scotty," she said. "There isn't any Den in this neighborhood. There aren't any Cubs at all."

## Chapter 3

## BOB AND HIS GANG

Scotty's lunch was a sad affair. Although his mother had tried extra hard to have his favorite food, Scotty couldn't eat. He could open his mouth if he tried, and he could bite, and he could chew, but he couldn't swallow. His throat had shut the gate to his stomach.

No Cubs. *This* was the fine new town they had moved to. Boy!

Scotty stared out of the kitchen window at the tree in his back yard. Mom said he could have a tree house. But what was the use of a tree house if there wasn't anyone to share it with? What good was anything if you didn't have some friends?

"What are you thinking about, Scotty?" his mother asked.

"I was just wondering," Scotty said. "I was just wondering . . . Why did we have to move, Mom? Why did we have to move?"

Scotty knew the answer, but he wanted to hear it again. His father had a better job in the new town, and would be able to give the family a better home, and if he made good, his company would give him a big promotion.

"So you see," Scotty's mother said, "this is Dad's big chance, and we have to help him. If we're not happy here, Dad won't stay. It would be a shame if we had to turn back now."

"I guess you're right, Mom," Scotty said. "I know there are other boys around, and I'll meet them sooner or later. It will be all right."

"Thanks, Scotty," his mother said. "I know it isn't easy for you."

When Scotty went out again after lunch there was one little thought that kept nagging at him. His mother had said they might move back to the old home if he wasn't happy. Of course he wanted his Dad to make good in the new town, but a fellow couldn't be happy just by saying it. Maybe he never would be happy in the new house, and they'd go back to the old place. Boy, that would be *wonderful* . . . except for his Dad.

Well, Scotty decided as he mounted his bike again, he'd like to be happy so his

Dad would stay in the new town. And if he found he *was* happy he wouldn't complain. But he was pretty sure he never would be happy, and he wasn't going to go out of his way to feel happy. Then maybe they'd move back where he belonged, and he sure would be happy then!

Scotty was coasting along the sidewalk on his bike, dreaming of how nice it would be to go back to his real home. He saw the rope lying on the sidewalk in front of him, and was going to run over it, when he noticed that it was moving.

Scotty jammed on his brakes just as the rope was lifted to the level of his handlebars. His back wheel skidded around and he had to put one foot down to keep from tumbling. By the time he had regained his balance he discovered he had company.

The two boys who had been holding the rope came out from behind their trees.

Scotty looked at them silently. At last he had found boys his own age . . . and trouble.

The two boys were dressed much like Scotty, in blue jeans and plaid shirts. One was a little larger than Scotty, and the other a little smaller. The larger one had dark hair and the smaller one was blond. But the way they looked at him was the same. Scotty could tell they were looking for a fight. He held on to his bicycle and waited.

The larger boy spoke first. He moved to within a few feet of Scotty and tried to stare Scotty down.

"Who are you, kid?" the boy asked. "Who said you could ride on this street?"

"Yeah," the smaller boy said. "We'd like to know."

"My name's William Roger Scott," Scotty said. "We just moved here." He added hopefully, "My friends call me Scotty."

The larger boy moved closer. "You don't have any friends around here. Understand?"

Scotty wasn't afraid of the boys, but he didn't want to get into a fight the first day. That way he'd never have any friends. And he wanted to have friends so much he was able to push back his anger at being bullied.

"I'd like to have some friends," Scotty said, looking straight at the boys.

The larger boy scowled. "You'll have friends when I say so. I run this neighborhood, and I decide who makes friends. Understand?"

The smaller boy pushed forward. "You want to fight?" he challenged Scotty, doubling his fists.

The larger boy pushed him away. "Who told you to butt in? I'm the one who asks first, understand? Get back before I let you have one in the eye."

The larger boy looked Scotty over carefully, noting that Scotty looked pretty husky. "You want to fight me?" he asked.

"I don't see why," Scotty said.

"Yellow!" the smaller boy screeched. "He's yellow!"

"Is that right?" the larger boy asked. "Are you yellow?"

"No," Scotty said quietly.

"Oh," the boy said, trying to work up a rage. "So you're calling my friend a liar, are you? I'll beat you up for that."

"If you really want to fight," Scotty said, "I'll fight you. I've got a new set of boxing gloves in my house. We'll go down in my basement and fight."

"Boxing gloves!" the smaller boy yelled. "Did you hear that, Bob? He's got boxing gloves!"

The larger boy, Bob, looked annoyed. "I heard him," he grumbled. He looked at Scotty again. "What else you got?" he demanded. "Any guns?"

"No guns," Scotty said, "but I have an archery set, and a lot of things I made in Cubs."

"What's Cubs?" the smaller boy demanded.

"Cub Scouts," Scotty said. "I used to belong in the other town I lived in. We used to make all kinds of things and have a lot of fun. One time . . ."

"Never mind about that," Bob interrupted. "We don't have any Scouts here. If you want me to play with your things you have to belong to my gang, doesn't he, Tommy?"

"That's right," the smaller boy said. "Around here everybody has to do what Bob says or they can't play."

"You want to join my gang?" Bob asked.

Scotty hesitated. Before he could answer, Bob answered for him.

"You better say yes," Bob said. "You don't get two chances. You're going to be in my gang. Only first you have to go through the initiation. If you don't do what I say, nobody around here will play with you. Understand?"

Scotty nodded. What else could he do, he wondered. He couldn't be all by himself. And if the other kids were in Bob's gang, he might as well join. Nothing was worse than being alone all the time. Nothing.

"All right," Bob said. "Now we're going to make you part of the gang. The first thing you have to do is get a string and a can, and tie the can to the tail of that black-and-white pup you were playing with this morning."

# Chapter 4

## SCOTTY'S INITIATION

"I can't do that," Scotty said, shaking his head.

"What?" Bob demanded.

"I can't hurt a dog," Scotty said. "I don't believe in being mean to animals. Why, if a Cub Scout ever . . ."

"Forget Cub Scouts," Bob said. "You're joining my gang. And you have to do what I said to prove you're brave enough to be in the gang."

"I won't do it," Scotty said, remembering the friendly little pup.

"You better do what Bob says," Tommy said. "Or else nobody around here will ever play with you."

"I don't care," Scotty said. "I won't be mean to the dog." He was hoping against hope they would find something else for him to do to prove his bravery.

"You don't have to be *mean* to the dog," Bob said. "All you have to do is tie a little old can on his tail for a minute. It's the initiation the gang has. And you know you have to do things like that when you get *initiated.*"

"Sure," Tommy said. "We all had to be enisiated when we joined the gang."

Scotty looked from Tommy to Bob. They seemed serious about the initiation. It wasn't the right thing to do, but he wouldn't hurt the dog. And he'd never have to do anything like that again. Just once wouldn't hurt. And he'd be very careful with the dog. A fellow *had* to have friends. And it wasn't always easy to get friends.

Scotty looked down at the ground. He thought of what Fred and Gary would think of him if they knew what he might do. If they could see him now! Cub Scout Scotty, the friend of the weak and helpless, about to tie a can on a dog's tail!

Scotty lifted his head, his eyes dull. Well, these boys weren't Fred and Gary, and there weren't any Cub Scouts to be found. He had to live with the kids in this new town the way they were. If he wanted friends at all, he'd have to be like them.

"Well?" Bob demanded impatiently.

Scotty looked at the ground again. When

he spoke, his voice was low, his tone one of defeat. "Let's find a can and some string," he muttered.

A few minutes later Bob and Tommy were hiding in the bushes as Scotty stalked the tan and white pup.

Scotty carried a small tin can and a length of string, and he approached the dog cautiously, so the owner wouldn't see him.

"Here, pup," Scotty called softly, feeling tears in his eyes at the betrayal he planned. "H-here, nice little pup . . ."

The little dog heard Scotty and bounded toward him with bright little cries of joy. Scotty held out his arms and the dog hopped into them, glad to be held and petted.

"Nice little feller," Scotty crooned, petting the dog softly. "Nice little feller."

"Come on!" Bob hissed from his hiding place. "Get it over with." He nudged Tommy and they both giggled.

Scotty fumbled with the string. "Listen, pup," he whispered. "Try to understand, boy. I have to tie the can to your tail. It won't hurt, boy. I'll tie it real loose so it will fall right off. Honest I will. I'm your friend, puppy. I . . . I have to do this to you so I'll have friends. I'm new here, pup. I have to do what they tell me to. Just once, little pup. Just once."

While he talked softly, trying to pet the pup with one hand, Scotty was slipping the loop of string over the end of the dog's tail with the other. Once he paused, ready to give up the whole terrible thing, but Bob was watching, and wouldn't let him stop.

Scotty's hand was shaking as he began to

draw the loop just tight enough to hold, but loose enough to fall off when the little dog ran off.

Everything would have been perfect but for one sudden turn of events. Just at the moment Scotty was going to let the dog go, the woman who owned the pup came out on her porch to look for him.

The moment the woman appeared Scotty shrank back. But at the same moment the pup strained forward. As he did, it tightened the loop of string around his tail. The puppy yelped and leaped out of Scotty's arms. The tin can hit the ground behind him and frightened him. He ran toward the house crying in childish dog tones.

Horrified, Scotty got to his feet, not caring that he could be seen. He stretched out his arms. "Pup . . . Pup . . ." Scotty called.

The woman saw her terrified dog and Scotty at the same moment.

"*You're* the boy!" she shouted. "Now I know who you are! I'll see that you're punished for this. You young ruffian!"

Scotty opened his mouth to explain, but the angry woman started toward him. He wheeled and ran toward his bike, filled with sorrow and anger toward himself for having allowed himself to do such a mean thing.

Running, Scotty saw Bob and Tommy ahead of him, shouting with laughter. They had tricked him. Made a fool of him, and caused him to do something that was awful.

Scotty reached his bike, hopped on, and made a tight circle that caused him to head off Bob and Tommy. "I'm through with you fellows!" Scotty shouted. "You can have your old gang!"

Without waiting for a reply he turned his bike and pedaled down the street.

"Gosh," Tommy said wistfully. "I was hoping to play with his stuff. Now he's gone."

Bob chuckled. "He'll be back," Bob said wisely. "Sooner than he thinks."

"How do you know?" Tommy asked.

"He's heading toward Luke's territory," Bob said. "Luke saw him playing with us, and he'll think Scotty is one of our gang. And you know how Luke treats our fellows when he catches them alone."

"Luke's awful mean," Tommy said. "Why he's almost as mea . . . as tough as you are, Bob."

"Yes sir," Bob said. "Scotty is riding into the hornet's nest right now. He'll be glad to come back to us, Tommy. Mighty glad. When Luke gets through with him."

# Chapter 5

## LUKE'S GANG
## —AND TROUBLE

Scotty was furious as he pedaled away from Bob and Tommy. He was angry with them, but even more angry with himself about what he had done.

He worked off some of his anger with hard riding, and it was when he slowed down that "they" caught up with him. Before Scotty was aware that anything was happening, three boys on bikes had him boxed in, and forced him to a halt.

The leader of the three was a stocky boy with red hair. While the two other boys blocked Scotty's escape path the red-haired boy advanced on him.

"Looks like we caught one of Bob's spies," the red-haired boy said. He scowled at Scotty. "Why did Bob send you up here to spy on us?"

"I'm not a spy," Scotty said, still angry over the dog incident. "And nobody sent me here."

"We saw you with Bob," the red-haired boy said. "That means you're with his gang."

Scotty sighed heavily and explained once again that he was new in the neighborhood and he didn't belong to *anybody's* gang. When he finished, the red-haired boy looked thoughtful.

"My name is Luke," the boy said. "What I say goes around here. If you want to get along, you'll have to join my gang and do what I say."

"Yeah," one of the boys chimed in. "Luke runs this neighborhood."

"He doesn't run me," Scotty said defiantly. "I'm not joining."

"That means he's in Bob's gang," another boy said. "Let's teach him a lesson."

"I don't belong to anybody's gang!" Scotty said hotly. "And if you think you can teach me a lesson, you just try!"

"Come on, guys," the other boy said. "Let's jump him."

"Yeah!" Scotty cried recklessly. "I'll take you one at a time or all at once!"

Luke eyed Scotty carefully. "Wait a minute," Luke said. "I like this guy's spunk. If he can pass the initiation, we'll take him in the gang."

"No thanks," Scotty said. "Bob tried that trick on me. I'm not tying any cans on any dog's tail."

"Did Bob want you to do *that?*" Luke exclaimed. "That shows how sneaky he is. We don't work like that in my gang. Around here, all you have to do is prove you're as brave as the others. I do the things first."

"What kind of things?" Scotty asked suspiciously. "I won't do anything mean."

"Who asked you to?" Luke demanded with a secret wink at his followers. "You know that old man who lives down the street? The one who was sawing the tree?"

"I know who he is," Scotty said.

"Well," Luke confided, "he hates kids. And he hates us just because we are kids. Like everybody else around here. They always chase us. Only he's worse than any-body else. Now, if I ride my bike around his house, do you dare follow me?"

"Just ride around his house?" Scotty asked. "No mean tricks?"

"Just ride around," Luke said. "He'll yell and chase us. You scared?"

"Not of that," Scotty said.

"Follow me," Luke said, getting on his bike. "That's all you have to do to be in my gang. Once you're with me, Bob won't dare come near you."

"All right," Scotty said. "Lead on."

Scotty didn't feel exactly right about the thing they were doing, but it didn't seem too bad. Just to ride around the house on his bike. And it wasn't right for people to chase kids just because they were kids. Look how the old man had chased him earlier, when he had gone down to watch the sawing. For no reason at all.

Riding behind Luke, Scotty swooped down on the old man's house. Luke sped across the front lawn and around to the side, with Scotty following in his tracks. As they raced by the side of the house Luke let out a long, loud mocking yell. In his excitement, Scotty echoed the yell. Then they were in the back yard.

Scotty was following Luke so fast that he didn't have time to brake before he realized Luke was leading him through the old man's garden. But brake Scotty did when he saw the rows of vegetables under his wheels. And braking, he did more damage than if he had ridden on.

Scotty's rear wheel slid out from under him and he tumbled among the bean rows.

Just then the old man burst out of the back door of the house waving his stick and shouting. Scotty threw one quick look at the angry man, and hopping on his bike he escaped over the garden. This was no time to stop and apologize or explain.

"New boy, are you?" the old man cried. "And worse than the others, too! If I ever get my hands on you . . .!"

Up the street Luke and his friends were hooting with laughter at Scotty. He rode past them without a word and headed for home.

This was the end. He was through with this town. The kids were no good and the grown-ups were all mean. He'd never be happy in this place. Never! The only thing to do was pack up and move back to the old home.

Scotty parked his bike in the garage and walked into the house. His mother was talking on the phone, so he went into his room where he found a book. He lay down on his bed and began to read, but the words didn't make sense. All he could think about was the awful place they had moved to.

A few minutes later Scotty's mother came into the room. Her expression was troubled. "Scotty," she said. "I want to have a talk with you. The neighbors have been calling about some . . . things they said you did."

Scotty didn't look up.

"Scotty . . . Did you . . .?"

Scotty sighed. "I guess I did, Mom."

"But why, Scotty? It's not like you to tie a can on a dog's . . ."

"*Please,* Mom," Scotty begged. "Please don't talk about it."

"I have to," his mother said. "Why, Scotty?"

Scotty shook his head. "I don't know," he said. "I don't know. It's the place we moved to, Mom. It's . . . Mom, please ask Dad to move back to our other house. I hate it here. I'll never like it. I don't want to join anybody's gang. I want to go home and belong to the Cubs!"

## Chapter 6

## ANYONE FOR CUB SCOUTS?

"Well, now," Scotty's mother said thoughtfully, "it wouldn't be very fair to Dad if we gave up without a fight and moved away from here. Would it?"

"I guess not," Scotty said. But deep in his heart he didn't care. He wanted to leave.

"What do you think we should do?" his mother asked.

Scotty tried to look as though he were thinking hard, but all he was really thinking about was going back to the old home. "I don't know," he said at last.

"*I* have an idea," his mother said, looking determined. "If there aren't any Cubs in this neighborhod, I'm going to start a Den. What do you think of that?"

Scotty thought of the boys who would be in such a Den. Bob, Tommy, Luke and his friends . . .

Scotty shook his head. Those boys weren't the kind for Cubs. Not the way they acted.

"I don't think it will work, Mom," Scotty said. "The boys around here are pretty wild and mean. They're not Cubs."

"Of course they aren't," his mother said. "But they will be before I'm through. Somebody has to get the group started, and it might as well be me. Come on."

"Where?" Scotty asked.

"You're going with me," his mother

said. "We're going to visit the house of every Cub-age boy in the neighborhood and invite them to a meeting."

"They'll fight," Scotty protested. "They hate each other, and they'll fight."

"Not in *my* house," his mother said grimly. "They'll be too busy to fight. You know, the more I hear about the boys around here, the more I'm convinced they need a Cub Den right now."

Somewhat reluctantly Scotty walked at his mother's side as she started her rounds. He knew what the other fellows would think, seeing him with his mother. They'd think he had complained about them, and he was getting his mother to fight his battles. The very idea of that chilled Scotty.

They went to Bob's house first. The minute Bob's mother answered the door, her expression was one of defeat. "Good afternoon," Bob's mother said. "What did Bob do wrong now?"

"Nothing," Scotty's mother said. "My name is Mrs. Scott, and this is my son William. We just moved here, and I've discovered there isn't a Cub Scout group here. I'd like to invite your son to a meeting at our house tomorrow afternoon, to tell him about Cub Scouts and see if he will join."

"I'm all for the Scouts, Mrs. Scott," Bob's mother said, "but you'll never get a group going here. The boys in this neighborhood just don't get along, and never will. That Luke Shortwell boy up the street—he's a terror. Always causing trouble, and his folks won't do a thing about him. On account of him, I'm not even on speaking terms with his mother."

"Would you ask Bob to come to the meeting?" Scotty's mother said. "He might like it."

"I'll tell him about it," Bob's mother said. "But I don't think it will do any good."

When they left Bob's house, Scotty's mother headed up the street. "Next stop, Luke Shortwell's house," she said. "Let's see what their story is."

At Luke's house Scotty's mother introduced herself to Mrs. Shortwell and explained about the Cub Scout meeting.

"I'm all for the Scouts, Mrs. Scott," Luke's mother said. "I know they do a lot of good, and I'd like to see Luke join. But you'll never be able to start a group here. Except for Luke, this neighborhood is full of rough boys. Like that Bob Carey. He's always trying to pick a fight with my Luke. He'd wreck the club if he got near it. I'll tell Luke about your meeting, but I can't say if he'll come. Not if that Bob is going to join."

For the next hour Scotty trotted at his mother's heels as they went from house to house inviting boys to the meeting. Everywhere they were met with the same story. The neighborhood was filled with bad boys, and it was useless to try to do anything with them.

When Scotty and his mother returned home, Scotty was discouraged, but his mother wasn't.

"I don't care what people say," his mother said. "I don't believe the boys around here are bad. From what I've heard, it seems to me no one has taken enough interest in them to give them anything good to do. And that's where Cubbing will help. Now, Scotty, we'll fix up our basement for tomorrow, when we'll hold our first meeting."

Scotty and his mother worked for the rest of the afternoon to get the basement ready. In the evening his father helped too. They arranged boxes for seats, set up a table with exhibits of the handicraft Scotty had done in Cubs, put up a flag in the corner, and tried to make the place look as attractive and interesting as they knew how.

"Tomorrow," Scotty's mother said, "things will start to be different around here. I've got some pretty good projects in mind for our new Cubs; I think we'll have a real good Den here before long."

The next day was also a busy one. Scotty's mother pressed his Cub Scout uniform while Scotty ran errands to get ice cream and cookies for the treat that was a part of every Den meeting. Scotty's mother prepared a small talk to explain Cubbing, and Scotty figured out a few words to say that would tell the boys why he liked to be a Cub.

Then it was time for the meeting.

The boys had been invited to come at three. By two-thirty Scotty had on his blue and gold uniform with all his badges shined and gleaming. A dozen times he ran down to the basement to make sure that everything was in order.

"You see," his mother said as they waited by their back door, "All it takes is a little effort on someone's part. We'll organize a Den, plan things to do, and in a few weeks the boys here will be every bit as nice and friendly as boys in any other town."

"I hope so," Scotty said, peering anxiously toward the street. "But I don't see anyone coming yet."

"It's early," his mother said. "Give them time."

The minutes ticked by. Two forty-five . . . two fifty . . . three o'clock . . . Ten minutes after three . . . Twenty minutes after . . . Nobody came. Not even one small boy. Scotty wanted to say something, but he was afraid to even try to talk.

Scotty's mother stood up. "We won't wait any longer," she said. "We'll start the meeting now."

Silently, Scotty followed his mother

down into their basement. He sat down on a box, looking forlornly at the circle of empty seats. His mother sat on another box. He couldn't tell how she felt. She didn't *look* discouraged, but she didn't look very happy, either.

"Shall we start the meeting, Scotty?"

Scotty stared at his mother. Start *what* meeting? Was she joking?

"We will open the meeting with the Cub promise," Mrs. Scott said.

Scotty rose to his feet. His mother wasn't joking, and he understood why she had begun the meeting. He was the only one there, but he was a Cub, and there could be no giving up.

Scotty stood erect and held up two fingers in the Cub Scout sign. "I, William Roger Scott, promise to do my best," Scotty began in a brave voice. "To do my duty to God and my country, to be square, and . . . and . . ."

Scotty faltered as his voice rang hollowly through the empty basement. It was the loneliest moment of his life.

"And . . .?" his mother prompted.

Scotty shut his eyes to hold back the tears. "And to obey the Law of the Pack," he said in a thin, choked voice. "Mom . . . Mom . . . We bought all that ice cream and there's nobody here but us to eat it!"

## Chapter 7

## RUNNING WILD

Two weeks passed, and one day Scotty made an amazing discovery. He was beginning to feel at home in the new neighborhood!

After the failure to get boys to the Cub Scout meeting, Scotty's mother had tried again, but with no results. She asked parents to come to a meeting, but no one showed up. The grown-ups in the neighborhood were convinced that the boys were wild and unruly, and that nothing could be done to help them.

Having met the boys who lived in the neighborhood, Scotty learned how to get along with them. At first they tried to force him into making a choice between Bob's gang and Luke's gang. But after a few scuffles, Scotty won his right to play with either group according to his own wishes.

Once that was settled, he began to have fun.

Scotty soon found out that no matter where he went, he was going to be chased by grown-ups, even if he wasn't doing anything wrong. And since he was going to be chased anyway, he found himself teasing the neighbors just like Bob and Luke. He felt it served people right for being so mean.

The boys didn't do anything terribly wrong, but whatever they did seemed to irritate the neighbors.

If one neighbor threw out some old jars, the boys would find them, play with them, and finally leave them in another neighbor's yard. The boys were always finding treasures in trash heaps, and somehow or other the treasures always were abandoned just where they didn't belong. At the end of an average day of play, the neighborhood looked as though every trash can had been hit by a tornado.

When they had been chased from everywhere else, the boys always wound up in a big empty lot that was next to Old Man Taplinger's lot. He was the one who had chased Scotty the very first day.

The lot belonged to the city, and no one took care of it, and everyone in the neighborhood used it as a place to throw old, unwanted things. It was a weedy lot, full of cans and broken bottles, but a good place to play war and other loud games. No one minded the noise there—except Old Man Taplinger.

When the boys were noisy Old Man Taplinger would chase them, and the boys would screech that it wasn't his lot and they had a *right* to play there. Some boy would complain to his father about being chased, and the father would come down and argue with Old Man Taplinger.

Then Old Man Taplinger would tell what the boy did, and the boy's father would be angry, and ready to spank his son. And at that time, of course, the son blamed another boy. Then the other boy went home and complained he had been accused of something he didn't do.

That was the way it went, with the result that the neighborhood was always in an uproar, and everybody was angry with everybody else.

Scotty never complained to his father. He knew how much the new job meant to his father, and he wasn't going to do anything to spoil it. He wasn't going to say a word about being unhappy. Because, in spite of all the troubles and fights, he liked most of the boys most of the time, and he was having fun.

It was after one of the typical noisy, quarrelsome afternoons that Scotty was relaxing in his room with a book. His father and mother were in the kitchen, doing dishes and talking, and suddenly Scotty was aware of what they were saying. His heart stood still.

"If what you say is true," his father was

saying, "I guess we made a mistake coming to this town. It *looked* like such a pleasant place to live."

"I haven't been able to make any friends at all," his mother said. "No one here speaks to anyone else."

"If we aren't happy here, we don't have to stay," Scotty's father said.

"But your job . . ."

"There are more important things in life than making more money. We want to live where we're all happy. As happy as Scotty seems to be."

"I wanted to talk about Scotty," Mrs. Scott said. "Ever since our attempt to organize Cubs failed, he's become like the other boys. I get phone calls every day about the mischief he's been in."

"That's the last straw, then," Scotty's

father said. "What good is it to have a better job if we're friendless, and Scotty is learning to be a ruffian. We'd all be better off if we moved back to our old home again."

Scotty stared at the ceiling, his mind whirling. Here he'd thought he was helping his Dad by trying to fit into the neighborhood, and look what had happened!

Now they were going to move back. His Dad would lose the good job.

Scotty sat up, his face grim. He wasn't going to let his parents move! He liked this new neighborhood, and he wanted to stay. And he wasn't going to let his Dad give up the good job, either! He had a plan.

Scotty got up and walked into the kitchen. His parents were standing by the sink, looking very serious.

"Can I have a drink, Mom?" Scotty asked.

They watched him quietly while he drank the water. He wasn't thirsty, but he needed a moment to get the right words in his mouth.

"You know, Mom and Dad," Scotty said, "I've been thinking."

"About what?" his Dad asked.

"About this neighborhood," Scotty said. "I like it here, but the kids are pretty wild. We're always getting into trouble. If we had a Cub Den . . ."

"We tried that," Scotty's mother said. "You saw what happened."

"Well," Scotty said, "I don't think we tried right. I know the kids better now, and I think I can get a Den started. And I'm going to start tomorrow."

"What's your plan?" Scotty's Dad asked.

"You'll see," Scotty said mysteriously. "Just be ready for a Den meeting, that's all."

Scotty marched back to his room and lay down on his bed. He could hear his parents talking again, and now their voices sounded more cheerful.

Scotty smiled, and then the smile stopped and backed up and fell down into a frown. He'd talked pretty big in the kitchen. But what if his plan didn't work? At first thought it seemed good, but now, on second thought, he didn't know.

What if the fellows all laughed at him, and hooted him down when they saw him? What then.

Scotty drew a deep breath. His plan had

to work. For his Dad's sake, for his own sake—and for the sake of his friends. It *had* to work.

But would it?

# Chapter 8

## SCOTTY HAS A PLAN

The next morning Scotty was ready for action. And he started by dressing for action—in his Cub Scout uniform.

Scotty's mother blinked with surprise when he appeared for breakfast wearing his blue cap with the gold stripes, his blue shirt, gold neckerchief and blue pants.

"Where are you going dressed like that?" she asked.

"Mom," Scotty said, "I'm going to get a Cub Den organized around here, and the first thing I want to do is show the boys what a Cub Scout looks like. I've filled my pack with some of our Cub books, and the things I made in Den meetings. Wait until the boys get some idea of what Cubbing is. They'll be around."

"Don't get your hopes up too high," Scotty's mother cautioned. "You know what happened last time."

"I know," Scotty said. "But this time it will be different."

Scotty didn't feel quite so cheerful when he finally shouldered his pack and left the house. What if the fellows laughed at his uniform? What if they thought the things he had made were junk? What if he couldn't convince them that Cubbing was fun?

Scotty shook these thoughts from his mind. He couldn't fail. Too much depended on him.

Scotty hadn't gone far before he met Bob, Tommy, and a couple of other boys in Bob's gang. The moment they saw him they broke into a yell and rushed forward to examine him.

"What's *that* you're wearing?" Bob demanded, looking enviously at Scotty's uniform. "Did you send away to a TV program for it?"

"Uh-*uh!*" Scotty said, shaking his head. "You can't get this uniform just by sending in box tops and money. You have to earn it. It's a Cub Scout outfit."

"What do you have to do to earn it?" Tommy asked, trying to figure out what Scotty's badges meant.

"Be a Cub," Scotty said. "That means doing Cub work and obeying Cub rules."

"What's Cub work?" Bob asked.

"Lots of things," Scotty said. "You take a Den meeting. First we get together and play a few games or sing some songs, or learn something about outdoor life. Of course we pledge allegiance to the flag, and repeat the Cub oath to obey the Law of the Pack and be square. Then we work on some project . . . Well, I'll show you. See this bone neckerchief slide? I made it myself. And that's not all. Look in my pack and I'll show you some of the other things I made. And of course we have picnics and parties, and . . ."

"Let me see that belt you made," Bob said. He examined a beaded belt Scotty had made with Indian designs. Bob looked interested, and a little wistful.

"I'd sure like to make things like that," Bob said. "I bet I could make better ones than you can. But my Dad won't let me touch any of his tools. Says I'll ruin them."

"Cub tools belong to Cubs," Scotty said. "And we make a lot of things. If you're interested, come to my house tomorrow, and we'll show you how a Den works."

"How about me?" Tommy cried. "Can I come too?"

"All of you are invited," Scotty said. "Any boy between eight and eleven . . ."

"We'll come," Bob said. "But we're not joining until we know more about it. And if we like it, we'll come again. Boy, when we get our uniforms, we'll be a real outfit. We'll give it to Luke and his gang."

"I'm asking Luke to join too," Scotty said.

"Then count me out," Bob said. "I won't belong to anything that guy is in."

"Have it your own way," Scotty said. "You can miss out on the fun if you want to. But anybody has a right to belong to Cubs. That's what makes it such a good outfit. We were going to have a hot dog roast tomorrow too. Sorry you'll miss it, Bob."

"My gang won't be there either," Bob said. "They do what I tell them to!"

Scotty looked directly at Tommy. "You can use my boxing gloves if you come, Tommy," Scotty said. "And maybe we'll have archery lessons, too. See you tomorrow."

Scotty lifted his hand in farewell and walked away. He grinned as a loud turmoil developed in his wake. Bob was shouting at his followers, and they were shouting at him. And it was hard for Bob to be tough, because he really wanted to go himself.

The scene with Bob repeated itself when Scotty met Luke and *his* gang. They examined his uniform enviously, and listened to every word he had to say about Cub activities. While he talked Scotty could see that they were dreaming of how they would look in Cub uniforms.

"It sounds pretty good to me," Luke said. "I'll come with my gang. But that Bob better not come around and interfere with our meeting."

"He won't interfere," Scotty said. "He wants to join too."

"Then count me out!" Luke said with an emphatic shake of his red head. "I don't belong to anything Bob joins."

"Too bad you'll miss the fun," Scotty said. "We were going to study animal tracks tomorrow."

Scotty saw Luke waver. He knew that

Luke liked outdoor life, and he had struck at Luke's tender spot.

"I'd like that all right," Luke said. "Maybe if I knew something about animals my father would take me fishing with him. I . . . I won't come if Bob is there. And I won't let any of my gang go."

That announcement was met by some open grumbling, and Scotty knew it was time for him to go.

"You're all welcome tomorrow," Scotty said. "See you then."

He turned and marched away with his head up, feeling proud at being in uniform again. The first part of his job had been done. Now came the second part.

With his heart thumping nervously, Scotty went to the house where Towser, the little black-and-white dog lived. He knocked on the door and waited.

"Well," the woman of the house said when she saw him, "what do you want?"

She hadn't recognized Scotty in his uniform, and was looking at him curiously.

Scotty removed his cap. "Ma'am," he said, "I'm the boy who was mean to your dog a couple of weeks ago. I didn't want to be, but I was. You see, I'm a Cub Scout, and we don't believe in mistreating animals. So I wonder if there might be some errand or something I could do to show you I'm sorry."

The woman looked at Scotty for a moment. "There is something you can do," she said, a smile on her face. "Towser has been cooped up all morning. How would you like to take him for a walk?"

Scotty looked up at the woman with his face radiant. "Oh ma'am," he said, "Thank you. Thank you *very* much! Just wait, ma'am. We're going to have a Cub Den here, and then nobody will be mean to Towser."

"You don't have to tell me about Cubs," the woman said. "When my son was your age he was a Cub, and I was a Den Mother. That was some years ago, and in another town. I've always wondered why they didn't have Cub Scouts in this town."

"We're going to," Scotty said. "My Mom is going to be the Den Mother."

"Well," the woman said. "If she needs any help, she can call on me. Meanwhile, you and Towser have a nice time together."

"We will, we will," Scotty said, taking Towser's leash.

"Come on, boy," he said to the dog. "Let's run to my house. I want to tell Mom the good news."

But even as he trotted home, there was a question in Scotty's mind. Would the boys come, or would Bob and Luke break things up before they even got started?

# Chapter 9

## A MEETING
## —AND A FIGHT

Once more Scotty and his mother waited for the boys to come to their house. Scotty was so nervous he couldn't sit still.

"Don't be too disappointed if the boys don't come," his mother said.

"They want to come," Scotty said. "But Bob and Luke might not let them."

"You know what's wrong with Bob and Luke, don't you?" his mother said. "They're afraid if the boys join the Cubs, they'll lose their leadership over those boys."

"Those two!" Scotty exclaimed. "Who wants them, anyway?"

"We do," his mother said. "They've already shown they have qualities of leadership. Now we have to teach them how to be constructive leaders. Some day maybe they can be Den chief . . .

"I never thought about it that way," Scotty said. He looked for the hundredth time to see if anyone were coming. This time, someone was.

"It's Tommy," Scotty said as he watched the boy approach. "Tommy's coming."

Tommy was coming cautiously, with many looks over his shoulder, and jumping from tree to tree to remain hidden.

"He's coming in spite of Bob," Scotty said. "We've got one recruit, anyway."

As Scotty spoke Tommy broke from

cover and raced toward Scotty as fast as he could run.

"Made it!" Tommy cried as he reached Scotty. "Where are the boxing gloves?"

"We'll get them out in time," Scotty said. "Let's see if anyone else is coming."

Again, someone else was. A member of Luke's gang was speeding down the street on his bike, hoping to go so fast that Luke couldn't catch him.

"It's Bobby Stokes, one of Luke's followers," Scotty said. "That makes two."

Bobby pulled up in the safety of Scotty's yard. When he saw Tommy he bristled, but Scotty was quick to enter the breach.

"I guess you two fellows know each other," Scotty said. "Even if it always has been from being in scraps."

Bobby grinned. "We have had our fights, I guess. Hi, Tommy."

"Hi, Bobby," Tommy said guardedly. "You going to be a Cub too?"

"You bet," Bobby said. "I want to build a space ship in Cubs. Like those Cubs do in other towns."

"I like space ships too," Tommy said. "That's what I want to build."

"You do?" Bobby was pleased from head to toe. "I never knew that. Maybe we could work together to build one."

Scotty looked at his mother, and she winked at him. So far, so good.

In a little while other boys came. Mark and Ralph from Bobby's gang, and then Harry and Warren from Luke's gang. Only the two leaders were missing.

As each new boy came, Mrs. Scott asked his name, then introduced him to each of the others, as though they were all strangers to one another. The boys nodded and grinned, then ducked their heads and waited to see what would happen.

"I don't think we need wait any longer," Mrs. Scott said. "We can go down in the basement and start our meeting."

Mrs. Scott led the way, and the boys followed her. In the basement they took their seats quietly, still acting as though they were ready to run out if anyone said boo to them.

"We'll pledge allegiance to the flag, and then I want each boy to tell the group what his interests are. That way we'll be able to plan a program that will be fun for everybody."

Scotty went to the flag and carried it to the front of the meeting. All the boys stood up and pledged allegiance. Then Scotty put the flag in a stand behind his mother's chair.

Next the boys took turns telling what they liked to do, and nothing they mentioned was anything like the things they *had* been doing around the neighborhood.

Tommy said he liked space ships and stories about other planets.

Bobby said he liked space ships too, but he also liked baseball, picnics, swimming, and summer vacations.

Mark said he liked to make things with tools.

Warren said he liked to take part in skits and plays.

Harry said he was interested in things like scouting and outdoor living.

Ralph said he didn't know what he was interested in himself, but everything the others mentioned sounded good to *him*.

"Well, boys," Mrs. Scott said, "if we can have a real Cub Den here, you'll have a chance to do all the interesting things you've talked about. And other things you haven't thought of yet, that are fun.

"Before we go any further, however, I think you ought to know what a Cub scout is, and what our goals are. Having fun is all right, of course, but Cubbing is the beginning of a long trail that leads to good citizenship. It will make you the kind of boys whose parents will be proud of you, and whose community will be proud of you. But most of all, if you become Cubs and live like Cubs, you will be proud of yourselves.

"Now, to begin . . ."

Mrs. Scott was interrupted by loud, angry voices at the top of the stairway.

Scotty ran to the foot of the stairs and looked up. There, at the top of the stairs, chin to chin and nose to nose, fists doubled, lowered lips thrust out, and eyes glaring, stood Luke and Bob.

"Oh!" Scotty cried. "Trouble, Mom! Trouble! They've come to get the boys— and they're fighting!"

# Chapter 10

## SCOTTY SAVES THE DAY

As Scotty's words echoed through the basement, the boys who sat around him suddenly tensed. For a while they had been part of one group. But now, with their leaders fighting, they were ready to spring at one another in defense of their "side."

Scotty knew that the explosion might come. Before anyone could move. Scotty looked up at Luke and Bob and bellowed at the top of his voice.

"Atten-SHUN!"

There was such strength and command

in Scotty's yell that Luke and Bob turned to look at him, their mouths open.

"You're late for the meeting," Scotty said, looking at them. "We've already had our opening ceremony. But you can come in if you keep quiet."

Luke and Bob peered down at the meeting. They saw their followers sitting side by side on the keg chairs, the flag, Mrs. Scott at her table, and Scotty looking indignant and in charge. Quietly they came down the stairs and found two seats as far apart from each other as they could get.

"Fellows," Scotty said. "I want to explain something. When we want quiet or attention from Cubs, we hold up our right hand with two fingers extended. Any time you see that signal, quit your noise and copy the signal."

Now that things were quiet again, Mrs. Scott explained the purpose of Cubs and how the meetings were organized.

"This Den is kind of a pioneer Den," she said. "If we set a good example, there will be other Dens formed, and we can have a Pack. So a great deal depends on what we do. I think we should plan a program for our Den, and then figure out what kind of project we could have that would prove to the community what good boys you really are."

There were a few gasps at that.

"You are good boys," Mrs. Scott said, looking around. "All of you. But it will take Cubbing to bring that goodness out where everyone can see it. Now, what about the program for our Den?"

Every boy had a different idea, and soon

they were trying to out-shout one another to be heard. But whenever things go out of hand, Scotty held up his hand with the two fingers extended, and the other boys, grinning, followed his example and quieted.

The first thing they wanted to decide on was a handicraft project for Den meetings. Suggestions ranged from whittling sling shots to building a rocket ship. But the question was solved by Bob.

All during the discussion Bob had been staring at Scotty. When the others had had their say, Bob pointed at Scotty. "I want to make one of those things Scotty is wearing," Bob said. "The thing he has his whistle on."

"You mean a lanyard," Scotty said. "They're easy to make." He slipped his off and handed it around. It was made of red and yellow strands of plastic fiber, with a snap hook attached to which he could fasten his whistle.

"If a fellow had one of these, he could carry the key to his bike lock, and never lose it," Luke said. "I'd like one too."

"Me too!" Tommy shouted.

The others shouted the same sentiments. Scotty looked at his mother.

"You've picked a good project," Mrs. Scott said. "It so happens we have a good supply of the plastic on hand. Just pick your colors, and I'll show you how to start."

A dozen hands reached for the colorful strands at once. As luck would have it, Luke and Bob grabbed the same red piece, and neither would give up.

"I had it first," Bob said, pulling with all his might.

"I did!" Luke answered hotly, pulling as hard as he could.

"Give it to me!" Bob said, getting red in the face.

"You give it to me!" Luke shouted, getting even redder.

"Try and get it!" Bob shouted back.

The two stood toe to toe, neither one willing to give in. Scotty held up his hand for attention, but the boys were too engrossed in the struggle to pay any attention to his signal.

Suddenly a look of triumph gleamed on Luke's face. "Here," he said haughtily. "I'll show you that I'm a better Cub than you are. I give you the plastic."

"You are not a better Cub than I am!" Bob shouted. "I give it to you."

"I gave it to you first!"

"I gave it to you second!"

Mrs. Scott took this moment to speak. "Boys," she said, smiling to herself, "it's nice to see both of you being so generous. And you'll both be rewarded. There's enough red plastic for each of you."

The boys took their strands and sat down, each one feeling noble. Scotty looked at his mother and rolled his eyes. He'd never expected to get over that without a fight.

Mrs. Scott showed the boys how to start their strands. But there were knots to tie, and they couldn't tie them alone.

"I need somebody to hold his finger on this knot," Tommy said. "I can't get it alone."

"Harry will help you," Mrs. Scott said. "Then you can help him."

In another minute the former enemies were helping each other, and the same idea spread to the other boys. Only two tried to make their way alone—Bob and Luke.

Bob and Luke gritted their teeth, fumbled with strands and growled like dogs, but they made no progress.

"Mine's coming fine now!" Tommy cried.

"And mine!" Harry echoed.

Bob looked at Luke, and Luke looked at Bob. First they glared, then they stared, and then they faced facts.

"Luke," Bob said, "would you hold your finger on this knot for me?"

"If you'll help me," Luke said.

"Sure," Bob said.

In another moment they were working together for the first time in their lives.

Scotty winked at his mother and she winked back. Bob and Luke were learning one of the first lessons of Cubbing. Success depended on cooperation.

When the handicraft period was over, Mrs. Scott asked the boys if they had any ideas for a good neighborhood project. They all thought very hard, and it was Luke who finally came up with the best idea.

"You told us that Cubs were like knights," Luke said to Mrs. Scott. "They went around looking for good deeds to do, and we can too. Why don't we be like a band of knights and go around the neighborhood looking for things we can do. We could help keep the neighborhood clean, and walk dogs, and give strangers directions, and all kinds of things like that."

Bob stood up. "I was thinking," he said. "There's that big empty lot next to Old Man . . . Next to Mr. Taplinger. If we cleaned that up, maybe the owner would let us play baseball there."

"There isn't any owner," Luke said. "It's owned by the city. I heard my father say so."

"Golly!" Scotty cried. "If we clean it up, the city might let us have it for a real playground."

Tommy jumped to his feet. "What are we waiting for?" he yelled. "Let's get to work!"

Luke bounded joyously around the room. "Watch out, everybody!" he cried. "We're on our way!"

# Chapter 11

## THE THINGS
## THAT CUB SCOUTS DO!

Luke's mother called Bob's mother on the phone. It was the first time they had spoken to one another in months.

"Mrs. Carey," Luke's mother said, "did you see what our boys are doing?"

"Fighting again, I suppose," Mrs. Carey said hopelessly. "It isn't always Bob's fault. Now your Luke . . ."

"They're not fighting," Mrs. Shortwell said. "They're going around with a wagon, cleaning up the alley."

"Our two boys?" Mrs. Carey asked, afraid to believe the truth.

"Our two," Mrs. Shortwell said.

"Imagine," Bob's mother said. "Well, I'm glad to see it. I always thought your Luke was a good boy."

"And I've always liked Bob. You must come visit me some afternoon, Mrs. Carey."

"And you, Mrs. Shortwell. Don't be a stranger to our house."

The lightning that struck in the homes of Bob and Luke struck other houses in the neighborhood. The telephone wires hummed.

"Have you seen what the boys are doing?"

"They straightened up the lumber in my yard."

"They rescued a cat from a tree."

"They helped a small child get his tricycle from the street."

"I heard them *singing.*"

"What do you supposed has happened to the boys?"

"I heard my Mark say something about Cub Scouts meeting at Mrs. Scott's house."

"We ought to visit her. She's a new neighbor."

That night Scotty lay in bed, tired from his day's work, but happy as he could be. He could hear his father and mother talking with visiting neighbors in the living room. Bob's folks, Luke's, Mark's, Tommy's, Harry's . . . They had all come.

And listening, Scotty realized his father and mother sounded happier than he had heard them for a long time. "Golly," he said to himself. "They were lonely too. I never thought grown folks needed friends."

He could hear what was being said, and it made him puff up with pride and joy. His mother was explaining how the Cubs were organized, and what they tried to accomplish. And she was pointing out that the best Cub groups were the ones where the parents helped too. And they planned to have a meeting of all the parents, and to have someone come down from the Scout office and show the parents how they could work with the boys to reach their goals.

Scotty heard Bob's father speaking.

"Until the Scotts moved here," he said, "our boys were always fighting, and in trouble, and we parents weren't friends. Now Cubbing has brought us all together, and we ought to keep it that way."

"It would help if the boys had a good place to play," someone said.

"I was thinking about that," Bob's father said. "And I have a suggestion to make. Bob told me the boys are going to clean up that empty lot down the street. It belongs to the city now, but it ought to belong to the boys. I think we should all get together and buy that lot to use as a playground."

"That's a good idea," Luke's father said. "I could send over some of my machinery later and level out some of those rough spots, so the boys could play ball."

"What I'd like to suggest," Scotty's mother said, "is that once the boys have cleaned the lot, and after we have bought it, that all of us, parents and Cubs alike, get together to fix it up. We could work first, then have a big neighborhood picnic to celebrate."

"That's fine," Bob's father said. "And I'll help the boys build the equipment they need. Bob has always wanted to use my tools to make things. Maybe I can teach all these boys how to work with tools. It's something they ought to know."

Scotty shook his head in wonder. He and the other Cubs hadn't expected any rewards for their work. Cubs didn't do good deeds for rewards, but to be good citizens. Yet it seemed that doing good brought its own rewards.

The next day Scotty and his friends gathered as usual to continue their clean-up project. They came with wagons and rakes and boxes and brooms.

Scotty didn't say anything about the empty lot. He wanted to wait until they had finished the work they had started. It would be a better surprise that way.

As the boys went from house to house,

Scotty noticed that they were being watched. Old Man Taplinger was sitting on a bench in front of his house, keeping a sharp eye on the boys. Scotty wished the empty lot were further away from Mr. Taplinger. Since it was right next to his house, he would probably be complaining about them all the time.

When the back alleys had been cleaned, the boys looked to Scotty for word about their next job.

"Well fellows," Scotty said, "I guess we're ready for the big job now."

"What's that?" Luke asked, leaning on a rake.

"Cleaning up the big empty lot."

"That will be a job," Luke said. "But I'm for it. Once we get the bottles and cans and junk out, it will be a swell place to play."

"And I'll bet the city will let us use it all we want to," Bob said.

Scotty grinned, but said nothing. He headed toward the lot, and the others fell in behind him.

On the way, they passed Scotty's house. His mother was outside, and the boys waved and shouted as they marched by.

"Where are you going now?" Scotty's mother asked.

"To clean up the lot," Scotty said. Winking at his mother he continued, "Mom, don't you think the city will let us use the lot to play on if we clean it up?"

Scotty expected his mother to join in the little game, but she didn't look happy.

"It isn't a matter of what the city says, Scotty," she replied. "Dad called about the lot this morning, and they told him that Mr. Taplinger bought the lot two days ago."

"Mr. Taplinger!" Scotty cried. "Oh, no!"

"That settles it," Luke said. "I'm not cleaning up any lot that belongs to *him.*"

"Me either," Bob said. "He always chases us. I won't touch his property. Not even for Cubs!"

"Oh, golly," Scotty said. "There goes our playground. And our ball field. These goes everything!"

## Chapter 12

## ARE WE
## GOING TO QUIT?

"No siree!" Luke said grimly. "I wouldn't touch that lot with a ten-foot pole."

"I wouldn't touch it with a *twelve*-foot pole!" Bob declared.

Luke scowled at Bob. "Who asked you to butt in?"

"I've got a right to talk," Bob said.

"Yeah?"

"Yeah!"

Tommy stood up and kicked his wagon. "I've got a good mind to take all that junk we cleaned up and throw it right back where we found it!"

"Wait a minute, fellows," Scotty said. "Wait a minute."

He could sense what was happening. This defeat might be enough to destroy everything. Bob and Luke might start fighting again, and instead of Cubs, they would have the same two old gangs again, with everybody always in trouble.

"Anybody can quit when the going gets tough," Scotty said. "Do we want to be quitters?"

"Why not?" Harry demanded.

"Yeah," Luke said. "Why not?"

"Our folks were going to buy the lot for a playground," Scotty said.

"If *we* quit our folks won't be able to help us. If we show them we can take bad news, maybe they'll try again, and find a way."

Bob nodded. "Nobody likes a quitter," he said. "I'm willing to keep on."

"Me too," Tommy said.

"Well," Luke said, "I guess we might as well finish the job. I sure wish we'd started Cubs sooner, so we could have had that lot for our own."

Sadly the boys trailed after Scotty, toward the weedy, junk-filled lot. Mr. Taplinger, sitting on the bench in front of his house, watched them approach.

No sooner had they stopped their wagons and begun to work than the old man rose to his feet and advanced toward them. "What are you boys doing?" he called out. "What do you want on my property?"

"We're cleaning it up!" Scotty shouted, ready to fly.

"What? What's that you said?" The old

man increased his pace, jabbing the ground with his heavy cane. "Who told you that you could come on my property? What do you want? Trouble?"

Scotty tried to frame an answer, but the old man was getting closer. He looked angry.

Suddenly Tommy lost courage. "Beat it, men!" Tommy yelled. "He'll catch us!" Turning, Tommy took to his heels.

Tommy's flight affected the others. Dropping their tools they turned and ran.

Scotty stayed where he was, almost too frightened to move.

"You'd better run, you young rascals!" the old man cried. "Broke my window, ruined my garden, stole my wallet! You'd better run! Shows you're guilty!"

The old man bore down on Scotty. "I'll get the truth out of this one," he threatened. "I'll get this one."

That was too much for Scotty. He backed up, turned, and raced away at top speed through the weeds. Once in flight he was so frightened he didn't know what he was doing. He fell over a stone and had the breath knocked half out of him. He pulled himself to his feet, expecting to see Mr. Taplinger right over him. The old man was coming at him.

As Scotty got up he noticed something made of leather near his feet. He bent down and picked it up. It was a man's wallet. Probably, Scotty thought, the one Mr. Taplinger had been talking about. He'd lost it, and thought the boys had stolen it.

Scotty held up the wallet. "Look!" he screeched at the old man. "I found your wallet!"

The old man didn't understand what Scotty said. All he saw was the wallet, and it looked to him as though Scotty was taunting him with it.

The old man brandished his cane in the air. "Thief!" he cried. "Wallet-rustler!" He hurried forward, shaking his cane at Scotty. "I'll teach you to steal my wallet!"

Scotty didn't know what to do. He wanted to give back the wallet, and explain how he had found it, but the old man was in no mood to listen.

Scotty waited until the last minute. His friends shouted at him to run. The old man shouted at him to stand still.

"Mr. Taplinger!" Scotty screamed.

"Honest, I didn't rustle your wallet! Honest!"

Then, as the old man rushed toward him, Scotty turned again, and still clutching the wallet, ran toward home.

# Chapter 13

## A REAL COWBOY

When Scotty came out of his bedroom he was dressed in his Cub Scout uniform from head to foot.

Scotty's mother looked at him curiously. "Why are you wearing your uniform today?" she asked. "Den meeting isn't until tomorrow."

"Well, Mom," Scotty said, "it's this way. I found Mr. Taplinger's wallet, and he thinks I stole it. I have to return it and tell him the truth. I just feel braver with my uniform on."

"I'll go with you," Scotty's mother said. "Would that help?"

Scotty shook his head. "I better do it alone, Mom," he said. "If you come with me, he'll think you made me take it back."

Despite his brave intentions, Scotty was shaking a little as he left the house. What if Mr. Taplinger didn't bother to listen, but started swinging that cane instead!

Outside, Scotty met Luke, Bob, Tommy and Mark.

"Where are you going?" Luke asked.

Scotty tried to sound cool and daring. "I'm going to visit Mr. Taplinger. Care to come along?"

"Not me!" Luke said.

"Me either!" Bob added.

"Well," Scotty said, "I'll see you fellows later."

"How come you're wearing your Cub uniform?" Mark called.

Scotty looked back over his shoulder. "Maybe I'll ask Mr. Taplinger to join our Den."

The boys laughed, but Scotty wasn't feeling very gay as he approached Mr. Taplinger's house. A dozen times he wanted to turn back and let his mother or father return the wallet. But each time he knew that it was his duty to return it just as he was doing.

He knocked at the door.

He heard footsteps inside, and then the door opened a few inches. The old man peered out, not recognizing Scotty.

"What do you want?"

"Sir," Scotty said, holding out the wallet, "I found this. I think it belongs to you."

The old man reached out and took the wallet. Scotty waited while Mr. Taplinger examined it. "It's mine all right," Mr. Taplinger said. "Some boy ran off with it yesterday. Had it hid in the weeds."

"Sir," Scotty said in a shaky voice, "that was me too. I didn't have your wallet hidden. I found it when I fell down."

"What?" Mr. Taplinger demanded sharply. "What's that you say? Let me look at you, boy."

The old man opened the door all the way and stared at Scotty.

"Say, boy," the old man said. "Are you a member of the U.S. Cavalry? You a Rough Rider?"

"No sir," Scotty said.

"You sure you aren't with the Indian fighters?"

"I'm sure I'm not," Scotty said.

"Funny," the old man said. "You're wearing the same kind of shirt and scarf I wore when I was with Teddy Roosevelt in the Spanish War. You're not my old sergeant, are you?"

"No sir," Scotty said. "I don't think so, sir."

"Then how come you're wearing our uniform?"

"Oh," Scotty said. "This is my Cub Scout uniform. Were you a Rough Rider, Mr. Taplinger?"

Mr. Taplinger motioned for Scotty to enter his house. "Was I a Rough Rider! Say, boy, I was the roughest rider they had. Let me show you my old uniform. Just like yours. I was a cowboy out in Montana when the war came. Joined up there."

Scotty's eyes flew open. "You were a cowboy? A *real* cowboy?"

"Sure was," the old man said. "And one of the best, if I do say so myself." He looked at Scotty with a hopeful expression on his face. "You . . . You wouldn't like to hear about some of my cowboy adventures, would you? A young feller like you?"

"I'll listen," Scotty said. "I'll never get tired of listening."

"Sit down, boy," Mr. Taplinger said. I'll tell you a few yarns about the old west, and every one is true. I haven't had a chance to talk about the old west for twenty years. Seems like folks don't care to listen to stories about the old days."

Scotty leaned forward. "I'll listen," he said again.

Mr. Taplinger brought out an old cowboy hat, chaps, a calfskin vest, a gun belt with two holsters, and a pair of worn cowboy boots with spurs attached.

"Those were my working clothes," he said to Scotty, sitting in a rocker as he talked. "I'll never forget the first time I wore those boots. I had to ride out alone that time, and it was rumored that the redskins were getting restless in the hills. Well, I'd heard that story before, and I wasn't going to let any redskins keep me off the range. I saddled old Patch, who was the best buckskin horse a man ever straddled, saw to my guns and ammunition, and set off.

"Well, sir, I hadn't gone a mile before I smelled trouble in the air . . ."


It seemed to Scotty that only minutes had passed before there was a knock on the door and there was his mother, looking for him.

"You've been gone hours," she said to Scotty. "It's time for dinner."

Slowly, with a sigh, Scotty left the Old West and returned to the present.

"Come back again," Mr. Taplinger said to Scotty. "Next time I'll tell you what happened when I set out to ride the wildest horse in the west. The one they said couldn't be gentled."

"Tomorrow," Scotty promised. "I'll be back in the morning."

"Don't be a bother to Mr. Taplinger," Scotty's mother said.

"A bother!" the old man exclaimed. "Ma'am, it's a pleasure and a joy to have this boy listen to my stories."

"Mr. Taplinger," Scotty said, "I'm sure the other Cubs would like to hear your stories too. We're interested in all the things you know about, like reading animal tracks, and outdoor living. Could I bring them too?"

"Boy," Mr. Taplinger said, "if they're like you, fill the house with 'em. I've got enough stories to keep you listening until you're six feet tall."

"I'll bring them," Scotty said. "But I would like to ask a favor."

"Scotty!" his mother said.

"What's the favor, pard?" Mr. Taplinger asked.

"Well," Scotty said. "Before we come in to hear a story, can we clean up the empty lot for you?"

"And I have a favor to ask," Mrs. Scott said. "Saturday afternoon we're having a picnic at our house. All the Cubs and their parents are coming, and any other friends in the neighborhood are welcome. I'd like to invite you, Mr. Taplinger."

"Madam," the old man said, bowing slightly. "I will be most happy to ride over to my young pard's picnic. And boy, you and your cowhands can work on that range of mine whenever you want to."

## Chapter 14

## THE YOUNG PARDS

"What's he going to do with that lot after we get it cleaned up?" Luke demanded of Scotty.

"He just bought it to keep us from playing there," Bob said.

"Let's tell him we'll clean it up if we can play on it," Tommy suggested.

Scotty shook his head.

"Look," Scotty said. "I want to use that lot as much as anybody. But our project was to clean up the neighborhood so it would look nice, and we ought to finish our job."

"Was he really a cowboy?" Mark asked.

"You should see his stuff," Scotty said. "All real western stuff."

"Well," Mark said, "if I can come and hear his stories, I'll clean up the lot."

"I'll tell you what we can do," Scotty said. "We'll ask him if we can play on the lot after we've cleaned it up. That ought to be all right with him."

"Okay," Bob said. "But you ask him. You know him better than we do."

The boys advanced on the empty lot. In a few minutes they were all busy. Some cut weeds, some picked up old bottles and cans, and others hauled the refuse away in the wagons.

While this was going on, Mr. Taplinger came out of his house and watched the activity.

"There he is," Bob said to Scotty. "Ask him."

"Sure," Scotty said. He went to Mr. Taplinger. "Howdy," Scotty said.

"Howdy, young pard," the old man answered.

"I've got a wonder in my mind," Scotty tried to say in a drawl, hooking his thumbs in his belt.

"What is it, pard?"

"Well," Scotty said. "My outfit and I have been wondering if we could play on your range after we get it cleaned up."

"You fellers are welcome to graze there winters," Mr. Taplinger replied. "Summers I've been aiming to have me a garden there."

Scotty's face fell. They didn't need it in winter. Summer was the important time.

He sighed hopelessly. "Well, thanks," Scotty said. "Guess I'll get back to work."

He trudged back to his friends. When he told them the news there was almost another revolt. A couple of boys were ready to quit right then, but it was Luke, of all people, who kept them on the job.

"I'm not quitting in the middle of the job," Luke said. "This place looks better than it ever has before. It makes the whole neighborhood look better. And that's why we're doing this job in the first place. Heck. If we get to play here in the winter, that's more than we ever had before."

Luke began working, and the others followed suit. Mr. Taplinger watched them for a few minutes, then went inside his house. When he came out again, he was wearing his cowboy outfit.

"When you fellers are through working, come to the ranch house," Mr. Taplinger called out. "I'll tell you about the time I was cornered by a band of Sioux."

It wasn't another hour before the work was done, and every Cub in the Den was sitting at Mr. Taplinger's booted feet, listening to a real adventure.

When the story was over, the boys hated to leave. They walked away quietly, with the past shining in their eyes. Scotty was the last to go.

"That was a swell story," Scotty said. "Will you tell us another one Saturday afternoon, at the picnic?"

The old man looked thoughtful. "I wasn't quite planning to come, son. Folks around here are kind of tired of my stories. I'd just be in the way."

"Hey! Guys!" Scotty shouted after his friends. "Do we want Mr. Taplinger at our picnic Saturday?"

The shrill cries of yes almost blew down the old man's house. He grinned and shook his head in wonder. "Well, I'll see about it," he said, stroking his moustache. "I'll see about it. I got some thinking to do first, though, young pard. I'm not used to having so many young friends any more. It's made me a little dizzy being around you fellers and not having to yell at you."

# Chapter 15

## EVERYONE FOR CUB SCOUTS

The Saturday picnic was full of surprises.

Scotty was surprised when Bob arrived wearing a Cub uniform. Bob was surprised when Luke arrived wearing a Cub uniform. And Luke was surprised when Mark arrived wearing his new Cub uniform.

Soon all the boys were in Scotty's back yard with their parents, and the boys couldn't get over the fact that all of them were in uniform.

"Boy oh boy!" Scotty cried. "Now we look like a real Den! This is wonderful!"

"More wonderful than you know," Scotty's mother said. "We've had inquiries from other parts of town about starting Cubs, and it looks as though we're going to have several Dens, and a Pack. The Scout office is even sending a man here for several weeks to get us organized and trained to carry on a real Cub Scout program."

"Wow!" Scotty exclaimed. "I'm so excited my throat feels like it's stuck closed. When do we eat?"

In a few minutes the families gathered around the long picnic table.

"I never would have believed this a few weeks ago," Bob's father said. "For the first time we're all friends and neighbors. We owe a great deal to Mr. and Mrs. Scott."

"Don't thank us," Mr. Scott said. "Scotty did this all by himself."

"Cheers for Scotty!" someone cried.

Scotty's mother looked around. "I hope Mr. Taplinger will come," she said. "I don't want anyone to be left out."

Mr. Scott stood up. "This is a happy day for us all," he said. "We had hoped to surprise our boys with the gift of a playground as a reward for their good work, but we couldn't. That's the way life is, boys. We get some of the things we want, and we have to do without others. I know your uniforms were a surprise to you, and I hope you will continue to wear them proudly. Every one of you earned the right to wear that uniform, and we're all proud of you. I . . ."

"Look!" Scotty cried.

Everyone turned in the direction he was pointing. Coming toward them was an im-

possible sight. A uniformed Cub Scout who had a leathery face and drooping moustaches.

Mr. Taplinger walked to the table, his eyes shining. "I thought I'd come in uniform like the rest of my young pards," he said with a smile. "Of course mine isn't regulation Cub, but it's the shirt and scarf I wore on many a chase after the Indians, and when I was with Teddy in the Spanish War. And if you don't mind, I'd like to keep it on."

As though they had received a signal, the boys jumped up and ran to the old man. They half-led, half-carried him to a good seat at the table, and tried to offer him every kind of food at once. The parents beamed and the old man laughed.

When everyone had eaten his fill, the old man stood up.

"Friends and young pards," he said, "I guess I have seen a miracle with these old eyes. And I guess I know how it happened, too.

"I won't try to fool you. I bought that lot from the city to keep these boys off it, because they were always tormenting me. That was my idea.

"When these boys started cleaning the neighborhood, I thought I'd see just how much bad news they could take and still keep working on a good idea. I told them I was going to plant a garden where they wanted to play.

"That's when I found out what kind of boys we have here. They were disappointed, all right, but they kept on working without any thought of reward. They did the job for the job's sake. Because it was the right thing to do.

"Well, now I've got one more thing to say. I'm going to have a garden on that lot, but not the usual kind. I'm going to grow boys there. These boys. Young pards, that range next to my cabin belongs to you."

When the shouting and cheering had died down, a dozen voices were heard.

"Now we can build playground equipment for the boys."

"We'll get that ball diamond laid out, too."

"At last they'll have a good place to play."

And a mother's voice: "We'll have to work out a schedule among ourselves to see that the boys get some supervision at play."

Again Mr. Taplinger rose to his feet, a noble figure in blue and gold.

"Don't worry about supervision," the old man said. "I live right there, and I'm home all the time. I guess my young pards and I will get along all right."

Mr. Taplinger hooked his thumbs in his wide belt. "Why," he said, "I've got the best way of keeping order you ever saw. Any time my pards get restless, I can always spin them a yarn about the Injuns in the hills."

"We could pay you for your time . . ." a mother began.

Mr. Taplinger looked indignant. "Pay me!" he exclaimed. "Ma'am, let me tell you something. When you reach my age, and you can have the company of near a dozen boys like these sitting around *wanting* to hear your stories . . . Ma'am, when that happens, you've been paid in full."

The cheers rang out again for the old man. Scotty stood next to his father, holding his arm.

"Well, Scotty," his father said. "How do you like the new house now?"

"It's not the new house any longer, Dad," Scotty said, looking around at the happy faces of his Cub friends. "It's home. The best place to live in the whole wide world!"